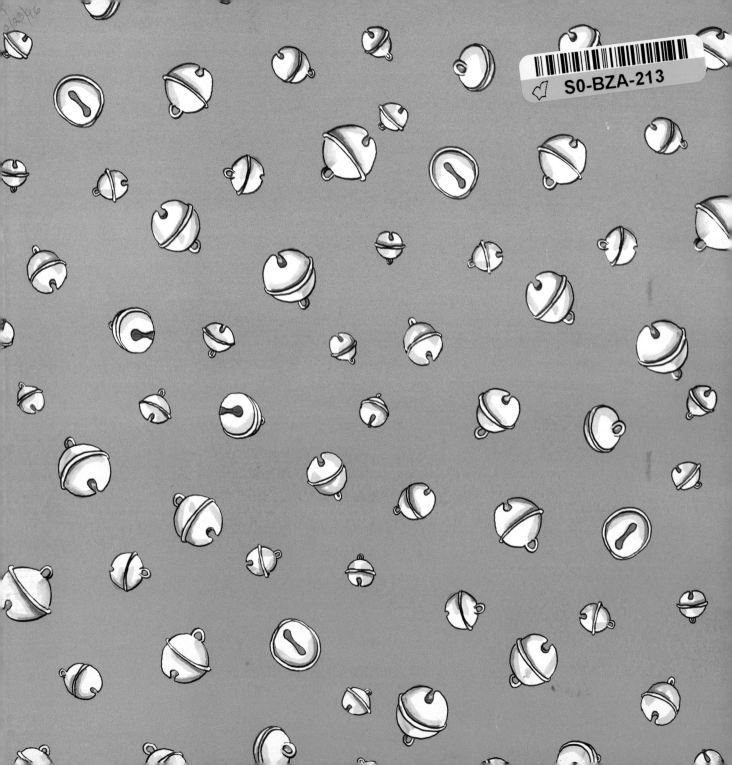

For Fergus

Copyright © 1995 by Anita Jeram

All rights reserved.

First U.S. edition 1995

Library of Congress Cataloging-in-Publication Data

Jeram, Anita
Daisy Dare / Anita Jeram. — 1st U.S. ed.
Summary: Daisy dares to do anything, but when her friends dare her
to take the bell off the sleeping cat, she hesitates.
ISBN 1-56402-645-0
[1. Mice — Fiction. 2. Behavior — Fiction.]   I. Title.
PZ7.J467Dai   1995
[E] — dc20   95-6305

10 9 8 7 6 5 4 3 2 1

Printed in Hong Kong

This book was typeset in Columbus.
The pictures in this book were done in watercolor and ink.

Candlewick Press
2067 Massachusetts Avenue
Cambridge, Massachusetts 02140

Anita
Jeram

Daisy Dare

CANDLEWICK PRESS
CAMBRIDGE, MASSACHUSETTS

Daisy Dare did things
her friends were much
too scared to do.
"Just dare me," she said.
"Anything you want.
I'm never, *ever* scared!"

So they dared her to walk
along the wall.

They dared her to eat a worm.

They dared her to stick
out her tongue
at Miss Crumb.
And she did!

One day,
Daisy's friends
thought of a really
scary dare to do.

They whispered it to Daisy.

"I'm not doing that!" she said.

"Daisy Dare-not!" they laughed.

Daisy took a deep breath. "All right," she said. "I'll do it." This was the dare: to take the bell off the cat's collar.

The cat was
asleep. That
was good.

The bell
slipped off
easily.
That was
good, too.

But Daisy's hands
trembled so much
that the bell
tinkled, the cat woke up . . .

and that was
very,
very
bad!

Daisy ran and ran
as fast as she could,
back to her friends,
through
the gate,
and into the house
where the cat
couldn't follow.

"Phew!" said Billy.
"Wow!" gasped Joe.
"You're the bravest,
most daring mouse in the whole
world!" shouted Contrary Mary.
Daisy Dare grinned with pride.
"Just dare me," she said.
"Anything you want . . .

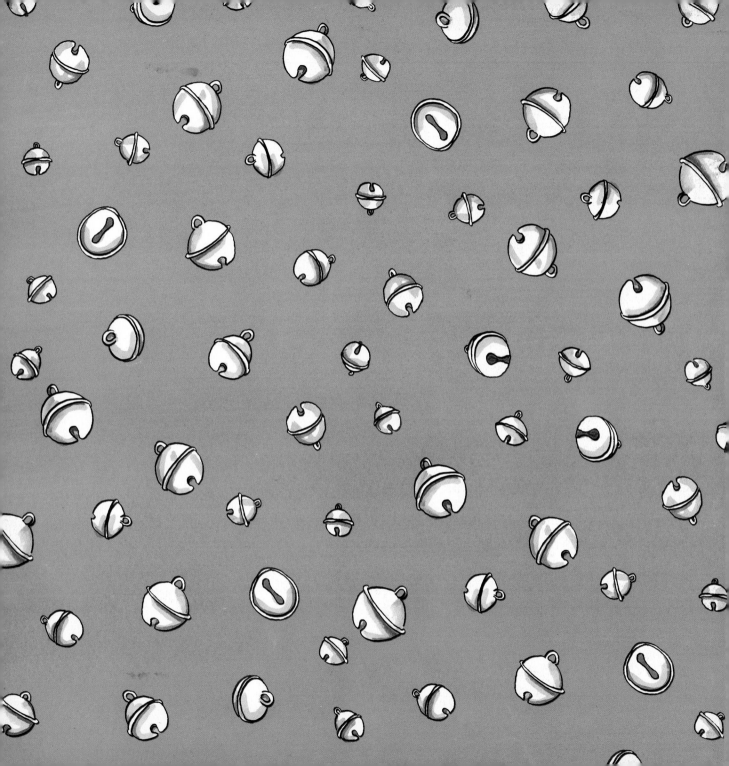